Help!!!

I Can't Dance Without My Bhangra Pants

Salma Zaman

Illustrated by Sahar Ajami

This is for Amaan

Dedicated to
Maleehah Zaman

ISBN: 978-0-9573285-1-8
Published by Salma's Bollywood Academy
Text copyright Salma Zaman 2018
Illustrations copyright Sahar Ajami 2018

Printed in England

Amaan was trying hard to keep up with the rest of the Bhangra dancers. They were preparing to take part in their local dance contest.

Suddenly, there was a loud bang!

"Are you okay?" asked the dance teacher, Miss Amber.

"I just slipped and tripped, I just cannot get these groovy Bhangra dance steps," said Amaan in a muffled voice.

"From time to time we all slip and trip," said Miss Amber, "but it is important that we pick ourselves up and carry on."

What I need is some Bhangra dance magic, thought Amaan.

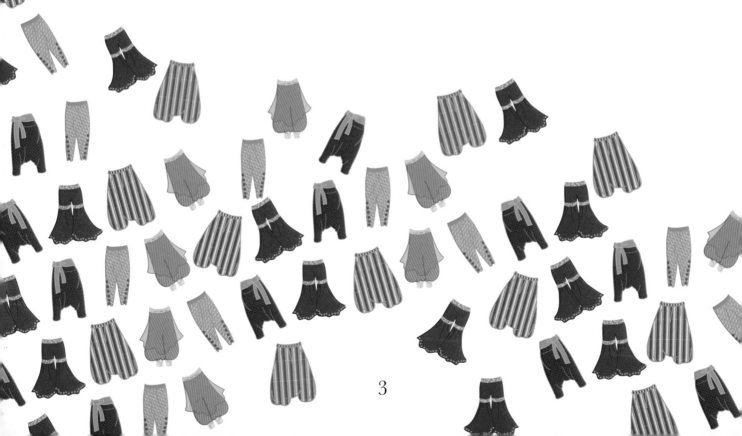

At home, Amaan explained to his dad how he kept slipping and tripping and how foolish this made him feel.

"When I was a little boy," said Amaan's dad, "I took part in many dance contests and, just like you, I was slipping and tripping all over the place. But one day my dad told me all about some pants."

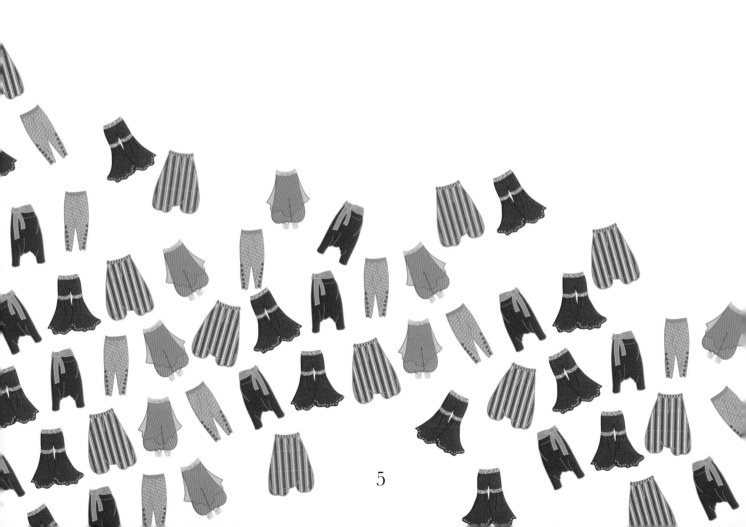

"Pants?" laughed Amaan doubtfully.

"Yes, that's right – pants. But these were no ordinary pants; they were bursting with Bhangra dance magic and when I wore them I danced without a slip or a trip!" replied Amaan's dad.

"If they were magical, did they help you win trophies?" asked a curious Amaan.

"Well, remember, it's not about winning – it's about taking part."

"Where are these magical pants?" Now Amaan was excited.

"In the trunk in the spare room," replied Amaan's dad.

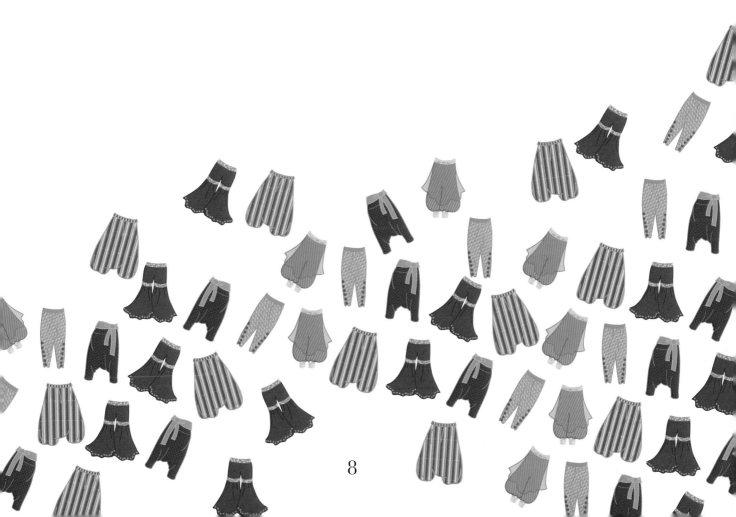

Amaan rushed upstairs as fast as he could. He opened the trunk and there they were, the most colourful Bhangra dance pants in the whole wide world, full of sparkles.

"WOW!" Amaan yelled, excited at the thought of dancing without a slip or a trip and getting some Bhangra dance magic in his steps.

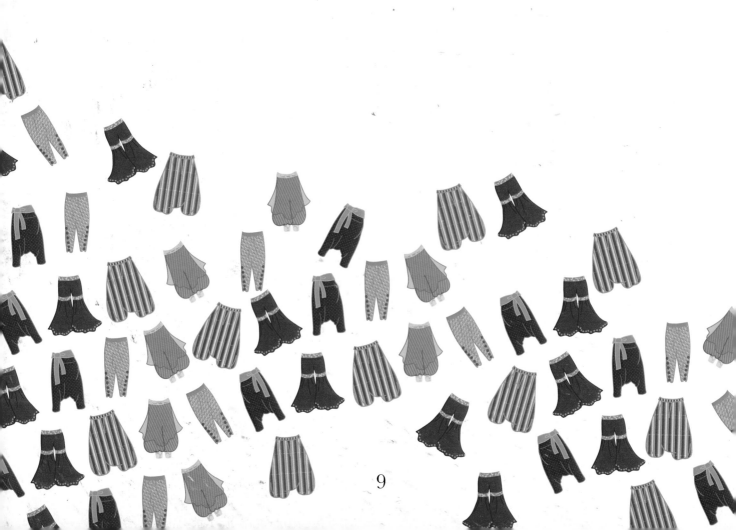

Just before the next class, Amaan put his pants on and waited for something magical to happen. He shook his body, but there was no magic; he twisted his hands, but there was no magic; he hopped and bobbed, but there was no magic; he yelled at the pants, "O balle!" but there was no magic!

Feeling deflated, Amaan was about to give up. Suddenly, he began to feel a tingly sensation all over his body and he felt like he was being lifted into the air.

"Wee! Woo!" he shouted as he felt the Bhangra magic all over his moving body. Amaan started dancing, managing even the hardest of the dance moves. All Amaan's dancing friends looked on in amazement including Lily and Roberta.

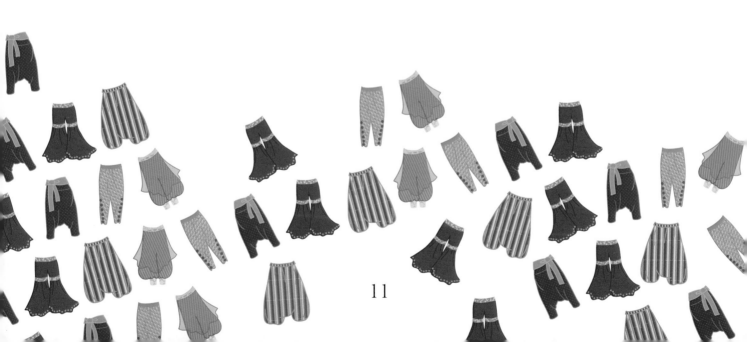

At the next dance class the dancers jumped with joy and bounced their Bhangra arms and shouted "shava shava!". They stomped from one foot to another, shrugging their Bhangra shoulders.

Roberta was feeling jealous of Amaan's new-found dancing skills. Since the dance contest could only have one winner, she had to come up with a plan.

On the day of the contest, Roberta put her plan into action and hid the magical Bhangra dance pants from Amaan.

It was almost time for the dance contest to start.

"HELP!"

"I can't dance without my Bhangra pants!" Amaan cried to Lily. "I have searched far and wide and I have lost my magic."

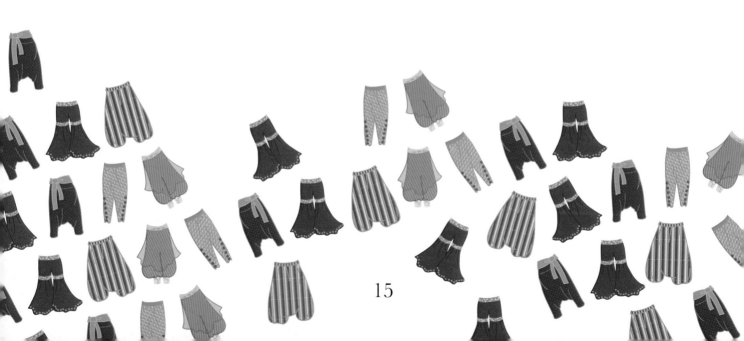

"You need to believe in yourself. We are all magical in our own unique way, pants or no pants," Lily explained. Amaan thought about what Lily had said and, like a true champion, hurried onto the dance floor.

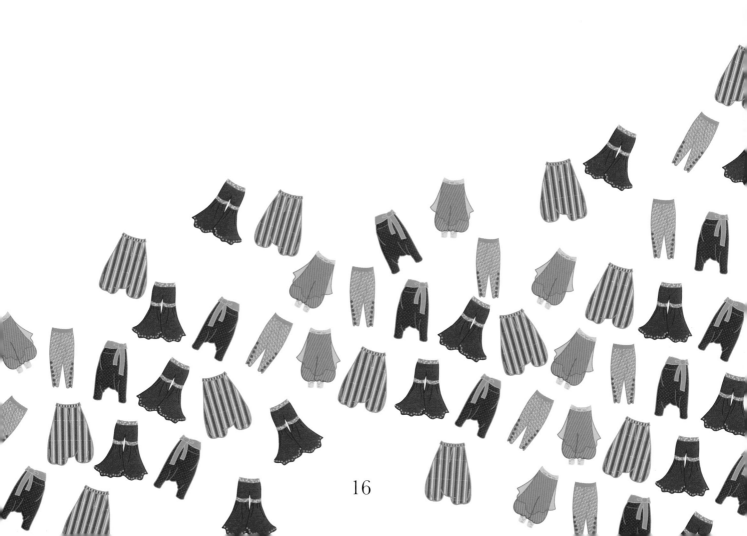

The dancers shuffled to the Bhangra beats. Amaan was performing confidently. Roberta felt her jealousy rise like a burning volcano and before she knew it she stuck her leg out, trying to trip Amaan over. But instead, she lost her own balance! As she was about to fall over, Amaan caught her – and even managed to make it look like the final Bhangra dance pose.

"Magical," thought Roberta. "We look good working as a team."

Soon, Amaan realised: it wasn't the pants, it was his dancing that was magical!

"The trophy for the best dancer goes to… Lily.

Amaan and Roberta cheered and clapped. They had both learnt how to be better dancers.

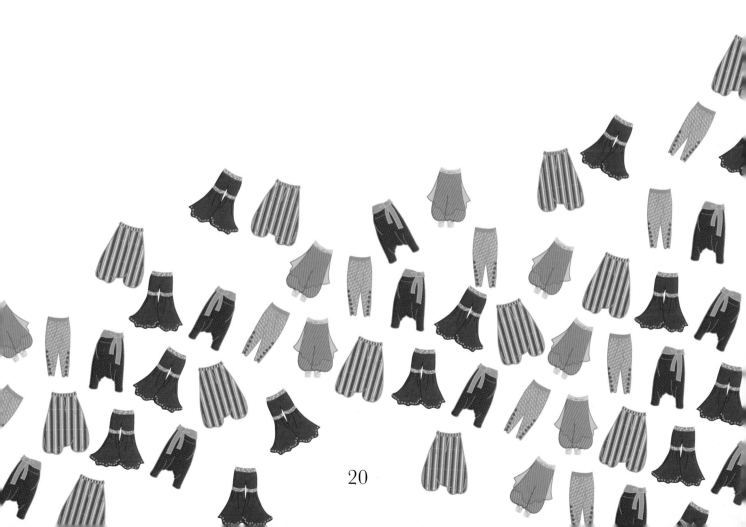

About the Author

Salma Zaman is a children's writer, bollywood teacher, choreographer, fitness instructor and the founder and artistic director of Salma's Bollywood Academy (SBA), the first ever British-Asian Bollywood dance academy for the North of England. Salma has been teaching for many years. She provides professional educational school workshops for all ages, levels, and abilities all around the UK and abroad.

As well as writing for her local paper, Salma has appeared on *Coronation Street, BBC1, BBC2, BBC3, ITV, Channel 4 - Identity* with Donny Osmond and choreographed and performed for bollywood stars. In addition, to this Salma has choreographed pop videos and worked on several British films.

For further information, to book author visits or dance workshops, or to order copies of any of her books, including *Bollywood princess,* please log onto

www.salmasbollywoodacademy.com

Or email us at

info@salmasbollywoodacademy.com